WE CAN READ!™

Freddy Bear

by Jacqueline Sweeney

photography by G. K. & Vikki Hart
photo illustration by Blind Mice Studio

BENCHMARK BOOKS

MARSHALL CAVENDISH
NEW YORK

For my brother, Michael, who was once
my Freddy and has now become my friend.

With thanks to Daria Murphy, reading specialist and
principal of Scotchtown Elementary, Goshen, New York,
for reading this manuscript with care and for writing the
"We Can Read and Learn" activity guide.

Benchmark Books
Marshall Cavendish
99 White Plains Road
Tarrytown, New York 10591-9001
Website:www.marshallcavendish.com

Text copyright © 2002 by Jacqueline Sweeney
Photo illustrations © 2002 by G.K. & Vikki Hart
and Mark and Kendra Empey

Library of Congress Cataloging-in-Publication Data
Sweeney, Jacqueline.
Freddy Bear / Jacqueline Sweeney.
p.   cm. — (We can read!)
Summary: Freddy Bear picks on Gus the turtle,
until the other animals show him how it feels.
ISBN 0-7614-1121-6
[1. Animals—Fiction. 2. Bullies—Fiction.] I. Title
PZ7.S974255 FR 2001   [E]—dc21   00-046865

Printed in Italy

1 3 5 6 4 2

Characters

Ladybug

Ron

Molly

Jim

Tim

Eddie

Gus

Hildy

Freddy

Gus needs help!" cried Ladybug.
"Follow me!"
The friends leaped, flapped, and hopped
down Pebble Path.

Ron yelled, "I see him!"

"Oh no!" squeaked Molly.

"He's upside down."

"Flip him over," said Jim.

"Hurry!" said Tim.

Everyone ran toward Gus.

"Eddie, you flip!" shouted Molly.

"The rest of us will catch.

One, two, three…"

"Oomph!" said Gus.

What happened?" asked Molly.

"Freddy Bear," groaned Gus.

"He flipped me."

"That's mean," said Hildy.

"Come on," said Ron,

"we'll walk you home."

The next day
Ron leaped on Pond Rock.
"Gus needs help!" he croaked.

"Again?" squeaked Molly.

"Yes!" puffed Ron.

"Let's go."

Eddie flipped Gus over.

"Freddy Bear?" he asked.

Gus nodded.

He hid his face.

"It's time," said Molly,

"to make a plan."

The next day
Freddy went out to play.

He passed Pond Rock.
Eddie wasn't sitting there.

He passed Willow Pond.
Hildy wasn't swimming.

Tim and Jim weren't hopping
down Pebble Path.

It's time to find Gus, thought Freddy.

He did not see Ladybug.

She fluttered into the woods.

Then he saw Gus.

Freddy ran toward Gus.

He leaped in the air.

But something leaped in front of him.

It was Eddie!

"Leave Gus alone!" he screamed.

Freddy ran.

He ran past two trees.

Out jumped Jim.

Out jumped Tim.

"Leave Gus alone!" they yelled.

Freddy ran faster.

He ran past Pond Rock.

Out jumped Molly, Hildy, and Ron.

Freddy fell down.

He started to cry.

"Tell Gus I'm sorry," he said.

"Tell him yourself," squeaked Molly.

"Here he comes."

"I feel awful," said Freddy.

"You made me feel awful too," said Gus.

"I'm sorry," said Freddy.

He reached out his paw.

"Want to go swimming?" asked Gus.

Freddy nodded.

Then Freddy and his new friends
went to the pond.

29

WE CAN READ AND LEARN

The following activities are designed to enhance literacy development. *Freddy Bear* can help children build skills in vocabulary, phonics, and creative writing; explore self-awareness; and make connections between literature and other subject areas, such as science and math.

FREDDY BEAR'S CHALLENGE WORDS

There are many challenging vocabulary words in this story. Help children begin to learn dictionary skills. Look up these words together. Read their definitions and then put the words in alphabetical order.

follow	reach	pebble	catch
plan	mean	croak	puff
nod	pass	swim	time
thought	flutter	toward	alone
past	fell	cry	awful

FUN WITH PHONICS

Many words in this story end with a "y" that gives them a special sound. Help children find the words that end with a "y" that sounds like "e," as in *me*. Have them write a letter of apology from Freddy to Gus for being so awful.

Here are some words to get started:

hurry	sorry	Molly
Hildy	lady	Freddy

PAST OR PRESENT

In this story, many words stress the past tense. Children can make simple flip books to practice using "– ed" at the end of a word to create the past tense. Cut five to ten strips of paper from any sheet of typing or loose-leaf paper, approximately two to three inches long. On each strip write the words listed below, staying toward the left side of the strip. Fold a two-inch section from right to left and write "– ed." Children can read the word on each strip, flip over the word ending, and read the new word. (If a word needs to have a consonant doubled before adding "– ed,"

be sure to add the necessary letters to the flip side.) Word strips can be hooked together with a simple binder ring. Here are a few examples: leap ed, yell ed, clap p ed.

leap	land	flap	hop
clap	flutter	groan	yell
squeak	cheer	puff	jump
nod	croak	shout	flip
ask	pass	start	happen

Locate these words with their "– ed" endings in the story and reread each sentence to be sure the meaning is understood.

FOLLOW FREDDY'S RUN

Gus's friends helped him to make a plan and to teach Freddy a valuable lesson. As an adult rereads part of the story (pages 16 on), children should draw a map of each move Freddy makes. Children can practice following directions and strengthening listening skills. Each step should be labeled. Map work can go a step farther, with the children drawing a map of a classroom or bedroom or writing directions to a special place at home or in school. Have children discuss Freddy's valuable lesson. What did Freddy learn? Write responses and begin a booklet of "Valuable Lessons We Can Learn."

GOOD GRIEF, GUS!

Poor Gus feels awful in this story. Discuss ways that we can help people to feel better. Children can make a list of "Mean Things Not to Do" and "Kind Things to Do." Adults can lead a discussion about other feelings, such as being frightened, sad, angry, happy, or relieved. Talk about how the characters in the story felt at different times. Create a matching game of characters and feelings. (All the characters from all the We Can Read books could be included.) Record character names on precut bear-paw shapes and feeling words on another set. Match the sets and discuss why each character felt that way.

About the author

Jacqueline Sweeney is a poet and children's author. She has worked with children and teachers for over twenty-five years implementing writing workshops in schools throughout the United States. She specializes in motivating reluctant writers and shares her creative teaching methods in numerous professional books for teachers. She lives in Stone Ridge, New York.

About the photo illustrations

The photo illustrations are the collaborative effort of photographers G. K. and Vikki Hart and Blind Mice Studio. Following Mark Empey's sketched storyboard, G. K. and Vikki Hart photograph each animal and element individually. The images are then scanned and manipulated, pixel by pixel, by Mark and Kendra Empey at Blind Mice Studio.

Each charming illustration may contain from 15 to 30 individual photographs.

All the animals that appear in this book were handled with love. They have been returned to or adopted by loving homes.

32